SPIDERS
IN OUR
BED

Spiders in our Bed
Jonathan W. Thurston

ISBN-13: 978-1-948712-70-5

© 2020 Jonathan W. Thurston

Sinister Stoat Press
an Imprint of Weasel Press
Lansing, MI
https://www.weaselpress.com/sinisterstoatpress

CONTENTS

CONTENTS

For Izzy, Sherayah, Miles, and any other arachnophobes in the world.

SPIDERS IN OUR BED

FOUR EROTIC HORROR STORIES

JONATHAN W. THURSTON

Sinister Stoat Press

SPIDERS IN OUR BED

FOUR EROTIC HORROR STORIES

JONATHAN W. THURSTON

INTRODUCTION

There came a glorious moment in my relationship with my lover Weasel when I realized that he was mortally terrified of spiders. He didn't like fake spiders, much less real ones. Naturally, when he came up to visit me in the fall of 2019, I had decorated my place for Halloween, with large spiders bigger than your hand and a couple hundred tiny spiders no bigger than the fingernail of your pinky. They covered the bookshelves, the dining room table, and the floor and walls of the bathroom. It could be expected then that when he had to go use the restroom at four in the morning that first night, he almost screamed from what he saw: a trail of tiny spiders going from his feet around the wall to behind the toilet, where webbing adorned the base. I might be a little devilish. As a result, this anthology is pretty much dedicated to him and other arachnophobes around the globe, like my friends Sherayah and Miles.

Me on the other hand, well, I enjoy spiders, of course.

My first pet was a black widow, and I kept her alive well beyond the max "wild" lifespan of the species. For anyone who knows my publishing house, Thurston Howl Publications, you would know its colors are red and black, my favorite ever since having my first pet. Further, my favorite toy as a kid was a Ty beanie baby named Charlie, an orange and black spider. I even got a tarantula when I was in college and loved the fuck out of the guy, a Chilean rose-haired named Venaticus. Needless to say, spiders and I have always been close. Hence, this book!

So, this collection is made up of what are called erotic horror stories. In my education, I have learned that erotic horror is best defined as a combination of both erotica and horror, thereby joining their purposes: good erotic horror *both* arouses and horrifies. It revels in taking readers to uncomfortable places of sexual arousal and then punishing the readers, making them either guilty for those feelings or implicit in the bloody crimes that result from that sex. This book attempts to capture those feelings. The first story is an arachnid twist of Stephen King's *Gerald's Game*, showing what all can really go wrong when you're "all tied up." The second story is a lot more Lovecraftian in nature, partially inspired by own lover's story about a bodysnatcher-esque retelling of one of his visits up here to Michigan, creating an all-new "sticky situation." Next, "Kill It with Fire" is a pretty common motto, especially when it comes to dealing with spiders, but sometimes the fires of passion and the fires of arson collide, at least in this story. The final piece is really a cautionary tale, reminiscent of *Scary Stories to Tell in the Dark*, reminding readers to "always wash your toys before use." The first story is one I thought of while having sex with my lover, and each of these stories really takes place in the same space in my mind: a small bedroom in a one-person apartment. The characters go by different names, but I would be lying if I said they are not based on parallels of my lover and I.

And now, with all this said, I want to thank you for opening this book. The pages that follow are morbid, grotesque, and all around not for the faint of heart. Be warned reader. Here there be spiders. They're between the pages, and they're under your sheets.

ALL TIED UP

"Are you sure you want to try this, mi estrella?" Daniel said to his lover.

Connor smiled and planted a kiss on Daniel's cheek, squeezing his hand. "Of course. I trust you, and I want to do this."

The two had talked about the possibility of putting Connor in bondage for a good couple of weeks now, but they were finally doing it. In their relationship, Daniel was very much a submissive bottom, and Connor was always the dominant top. They were used to Connor tying up Daniel, using toys on him, putting him in a chastity cage, and making him wear femboy clothing. They liked their dynamics in bed. But sometimes, like tonight, they wanted to try something a little bit different.

The idea had been Connor's originally. He had always wanted to know what Daniel got out of the bondage scenarios. Connor had no interest in doing much bottoming. He knew what he liked on that front, but he had not really been on the receiving end in a bondage scenario. So, the couple had decided to try a very basic scene: Daniel would tie Connor to the bed and leave him there for an hour or so. Minimal bondage equipment: restraints, light nipple clamps, a collar, and maybe even a gag. That was it. Just a little experiment.

"Well," Daniel said, biting a lip, "what do you want me to do while you're all tied up? Want me to sit by the bed? I could just read a book or something."

"Nah," said Connor with a shake of his head. "I want to do this right. It might be uncomfortable at first. Just take a long shower or something like that. Check on me in like…an hour. Sound good?"

Daniel nodded. "Ok, estrella. Lie on the bed, and I'll get started."

Connor obeyed. They were both already naked, and the gear was already set up. "I'm ready," Connor said with a giddy grin. It was both exciting and nervewracking trying something like this.

"Good." Daniel pulled each wrist and ankle to the corners of the mattress and started applying the restraints. Each one was a black leather with a softer fabric on the inside of the cuffs. They gave each limb about two or three inches of movement, and that was about it. Each of the four cuffs had a separate lock, securing Connor's limbs tight inside. "Still comfy?" Daniel said, after each of the four restraints were in place.

"Fuck yeah. This is easy," Connor replied, trying to convince himself as much as Daniel.

"Alright, let's get the clamps going next." He reached down to the bookshelf-turned-nightstand to grab the metallic clamps and then got onto the bed, straddling Connor's waist. Connor bit his lip hard, and Daniel laughed. "Goober." To tease him, Daniel rubbed his bare ass against Connor's semihard cock and continued until he was fully hard against him. Once he was satisfied with that, he placed the clamps on each of Connor's nipples. "How's that feel?"

It was definitely new for Connor, but they weren't too tight. It was a numb pain that mixed with pleasure. "It's nice," he said back honestly.

"Great! Next..." Daniel leaned back over to the bookshelf and grabbed the O-ring gag there. It was a medium rubber with leather straps that worked around the back of the head. The O-ring itself was thick so that it couldn't be twisted in the mouth. Daniel leaned forward again and kissed Connor on the mouth. When he pulled his head away, he placed the O-ring into Connor's mouth, fitting it snugly between his jaws. Then, Daniel lifted Connor's head up and secured the straps behind his head. He got off the mattress and stood over his lover.

Putting his hands on his hips, Daniel smiled as he admired his handiwork. "Not too bad if I do say so myself." He grabbed his cell phone off the nightstand and took a quick series of photos of his lover, even though Connor groaned and grumbled through the gag at him, frowning playfully. "Aw, c'mon. It's not every day I get to see mi estrella all tied up like this." He put his phone down and grabbed Connor's, pulling up the timer app. "Well, are you comfortable? Make one grunt if yes, two if kinda, three if not at all."

Ungh.

Connor mentally made a second grunt but didn't vocally express that one. He was tough. He could take a little discomfort. Since Daniel had worked him up first, his cock was hard and leaking pre against his stomach.

His nipples were starting to feel the burn a bit more, and his jaws were already aching a little bit. But he wasn't going to give in so easily. If his baby could take it, so could he.

"Good." Daniel stood Connor's phone up by the lamp on the bookshelf so that it was facing Daniel. The dense pillows Connor's head was propped up on didn't allow Connor to turn his head too much, just enough to see the timer. "I've set the timer for an hour and a half. I'm just gonna take a long shower. Probably gonna shave and stuff, and we can have some fun after. You can even tie me up before you have your way with me if you'd like. Or maybe," he said, leaning forward to blow a stream of hot air across Connor's dick, "I'll just ride you like this. Sound good?"

Ungh!

"Ha! Alright, I'll be back when the timer's out. I'll set my phone the same. Love you." He got up and stood. Since the mattress was low to the ground, its head a good foot below the windowsill in the bedroom, Daniel practically towered over Connor. He grabbed his own phone and left the room, closing the door behind him on his way to the bathroom.

Connor knew he was fully alone when he heard the shower turn on in the bathroom, followed only seconds later by the blaring music of Ke$ha's new album through the closed doors. Daniel always did like his pop music, but Ke$ha was at least something they both liked.

He found himself imagining Daniel getting all wet and sudsy under the steaming water of the shower. He imagined all the times they'd fucked in that shower, sometimes with Daniel in full pup gear, sometimes in just a harness, sometimes in nothing. It got to the point where, even when Connor showered by himself, he still naturally got a hard-on. He just couldn't help it. But for now, Daniel was in the shower all by himself, and Connor was tied to their bed for the first time. Part of him could see the appeal of this kind of bondage for a long time, but the other part was just begging to get out. He felt restless on the best of days; now he was tied down with literally nothing to do for the next hour to hour and a half. And the discomfort was just mounting with each passing minute.

He started squirming in his restraints, testing them. The cuffs around his wrists and ankles were tight, almost cutting off his circulation. He really felt it when he pulled on them. They had been tied well to the bedposts, only giving him a couple inches of movement in any direction. After about ten minutes, he felt the burn in his thighs since they were spread so far. His arms felt like they were starting to go to sleep, too. His nipples were what hurt the most though. How could anyone get used to clamps like these? Daniel hadn't even tightened them to their medium level. They were barely on, and they were already hurting like hell.

Nnf, he whined against his gag. He tongued the O-shape of the rubber and pushed his tongue through. He couldn't talk around it, but he could move his tongue just fine still. He could breathe fine. It just felt weird having such a thick object in his mouth, holding his jaws apart. He had sucked Daniel's dick a few times, but he had never just held it there for minutes at a time. Like his arms and legs, his jaw was getting sore as fuck.

He looked to his left over at the bookshelf and saw the timer. Exactly fifteen minutes had passed. He groaned and closed his eyes. *You just need to relax,* he told himself.

Time will pass by faster than ever if you just don't think about it all so much. Just...think about poetry you've been working on or what you're gonna work on later tonight.

It worked for a bit too. He opened his eyes and just stared at the far wall, near the door. He thought about anything and everything except his current restricted predicament.

Just as he was getting relaxed, he thought he saw a movement above him out of the corner of his vision.

His eyes flicked up toward the dark shape, and he squinted. There was something up in the corner of the window above his head. Whatever it was, it was moving, but its shape was partially obscured. When it moved again, he got a better look at it. It was a big, fat, ugly spider.

Now, if there was one thing Connor hated more than being uncomfortable or feeling restless, it was spiders. Fuck the fact that they were necessary for the environment. Fuck the fact that "not all spiders are out to get you." His philosophy toward spiders was simply and literally, "Fuck 'em. Don't fuck 'em, but fuck 'em." And this spider was no exception. Even though it was a good six feet over his face, he could see it was black and hairy with long legs that twisted at sharp angles as it walked.

Once it had moved enough, he realized what had been obscuring it from his vision. Nestled in the corner of the window was something just as big, fat, and ugly as the spider: its egg sac.

Fuck no, he tried to say, though it just came out as, *Ungh uh.* He tried moaning louder, trying to call for Daniel as he watched the spider fiddle with the egg sac as if it might be wrapping it up with more silk. Connor wasn't really scared the egg sac would fall or anything. He just didn't like the idea of that huge-ass spider just chilling above his head. He kept moaning, hopeful that Daniel would somehow hear him over the shower and the Ke$ha music.

Despite his moaning in complaint, though, the shower went on. The music went on. And the egg sac fell.

You know those movies where something dramatic happens in slo-mo? And you hope and expect the hero will stop it from happening? Yeah, that didn't happen here. The egg sac fell six feet down and landed at the edge of the windowsill, crushing itself on impact.

At first, Connor didn't think anything had really happened, even though he held his breath in his throat. The mama spider began walking down the glass surface of the window. But Connor wasn't really watching her. His eyes widened as he watched tens, no, *hundreds,* of tiny black spiders emerge out of the ruptured egg sac. They crawled down the windowsill.

Now, Connor really freaked out. All his limbs shook, making the bed almost hop in place. His boner was now officially dead, and he kept trying to angle his head away from the wall, but he just couldn't get it to move more than a few inches since his body was so well restricted and his head was deep in the thick body pillow. It didn't stop him from moaning wildly through the O-ring gag though.

His body bucked and contorted as much as it possibly could on the bed, his hips twisting this way and that in his frantic attempts to get away from the spreading mass of black critters now inches above his face.

His throat started making this high, screaming whine as the first spider dangled slowly from a thin silken thread, crawling through the air from the windowsill to land on his forehead. Even as tiny as it was, he could see its miniscule, jet-black eyes and the hairs that were sprouting on its legs. He felt its body land on his forehead, even as the mama spider had reached the windowsill.

His cock shriveled up against his body, and the cloud of baby spiders crawled down from the windowsill onto his head, weaving their way through his dark hair and spreading out across his tan skin.

He screamed louder, high yet guttural, a desperate scream. The spiders crawled over his face, over his nose, around his lips, down his chin, even going to his bare chest. He occasionally felt them brush over his sore and still very sensitive nipples.

Since his mouth was open, he could somewhat control air flow. Expelling sharp breaths, he tried to blow spiders off his face, but he could not angle the breath down his face or up toward his nose. It just went out, and even then, the breaths were weak, ragged. His skin felt alive with the prickling sensation of hundreds of spiders's legs running across him.

Despite his attempts at blowing at the spiders, he saw the large one, the mama, finally crawl down from the windowsill, her massive legs swaying in the air as she descended to his forehead, her pedipalps rubbing each other like the villain of an old movie rubbing his hands together with an evil grin. She landed on his forehead and made her way down the bridge of his nose.

As his screams rose in volume, she stretched her legs down into the O-ring gag. He felt her hair legs touch his tongue, and she slipped inside, her children beginning to follow her into the dark, moist depths of that fleshy cavern, even as the cavern screamed louder, those pipes opening up for the spiders' entrance.

Daniel kept showering, singing along to Ke$ha's "Grow a Pear," glad that his boyfriend was brave enough to experiment when it came to sex and trusted him enough to be the one he experimented with. He ran the bar of soap across his erection and smiled. He still had an hour left on his phone timer. Never happier, he lost himself in the steam, soap, and song.

A STICKY SITUATION

Raymond pushed his dick hard against my taint, and I winced. "Hey, a bit lower, babe."

"Oh, sorry," he said with a laugh, and he pulled his dick up. I rolled my eyes back in pleasure as his tip found my entrance. "I take it I found it that time," he said, not really asking, judging from my reaction.

"Fuck yes." It had been two months since I had seen him last, and the winter snow had started to fall in Lansing, Michigan. The frost glazed the window over my head, but the white light filtered in through the curtains over our enmeshed bodies. His breath felt hot over my cool skin as he pushed into me, inch by inch. Sometimes, I squirmed, and other times I pushed back, urging him deeper. To me, Ray was lover, mate, and Adonis rolled up in one. He had left everything to come up and be with me: family, friends, and his generational home. We were ready for a new life together. Well, at least he was.

He pushed in to the base and kissed my mouth. "That

feel okay?" he asked, caressing my cheek, my legs held on each of his shoulders.

"Fuck yes. Fuck me hard, daddy."

He smiled, and I moved my arms up to his face, stroking that perfect skin and scruff. "You asked for it."

He pounded my ass hard, no longer asking me if I was okay, instead reading my eyes and face for the signs of pleasure, and the signs were indeed written there, in every moan, rolling of my eyes, and sharp gasps. I was in heaven, and I felt that golden glow every time his balls slapped my ass.

As he found his rhythm, I moaned out in pleasure, urging him on. My throat felt dry. My gasps were so rough and sharp, I felt my voice failing me. But I still mouthed the word, *Harder*. Every time he pushed into me, I clenched around him, not wanting him to pull out at the same time I wanted him to thrust into me again.

He held the backs of my knees down toward my own shoulders and sat up more, grinding against me slowly but deeply. He smiled and grabbed his phone, holding it over us as he pushed into me. I must not have been moaning loud enough: once he started filming, he grabbed my balls and used them as a harness while he fucked me. I found my voice again and yelped in pleasure and pain. I heard him moan, too. He was enjoying this as much as I was.

After a minute and a half of that, he threw the phone down onto the bed, let go of my balls, and grabbed the balls of my feet instead, pushing them until they were behind the pillow, well past my head. While my limbs stretched and strained, my ass was raised, and his balls made an audible slapping sound with each thrust. His cock seemed to grow inside me, getting bigger and harder. His breath grew ragged, shallow, quick. Each puff of air warmed against my face in bursts of heat. His sweat dripped onto my chest, and I felt his pre frothing around his dick in my ass, lubing him up more. His cock throbbed against my prostate, and his thrusts sped up, staying deep but going faster, just slamming my insides hard.

"F-Fuck, Charlie," he started, spittle falling from his perfect lips onto my face. "I-I'm gonna cum."

I lapped up the spit that landed on my lips obediently and gasped, "Do it, daddy. Breed me hard!"

He kept thrusting, his head buried in my chest, until I felt his cock shoot load after load of hot cum into me. It actually felt unbearably hot for just a moment, and then it just felt comfortable. He gritted his teeth as the orgasm took over his body, and he slammed against my ass a few more times. I moaned sharply with each of those final thrusts, and my cock leaked pre all over my stomach from it. It felt great.

I could definitely tell from his energy—and how quick it was—he hadn't fucked probably since he had last seen me. And I was in the same boat myself. I had been super close to cumming myself while he fucked me. Every single inch of me was alive with pleasure. I was ready to go at least another couple of rounds tonight, but I knew it wouldn't be so.

He collapsed against me, spent, and I just wanted to hold him, embrace him forever and never let him go, but I knew this moment would pass...and it would pass forever. That was just the nature of things.

I was able to get my legs wrapped around his waist, and my arms reached around his shoulders, leaving thin scratch marks up his back. He gasped and shivered against me, his head lying on my shoulder.

"I'm dead," he muttered into my neck.

"Mmm, same," I replied, still completely horny myself.

"I don't know where you get the energy, babe."

I laughed. "Me, neither. But you knew what you signed up for!"

"Did I though?" he said sleepily.

"Mhm."

"Well, I think you're gonna be the death of me. You wear me the fuck out."

"Oh, c'mon," I teased, "I'm sure I could get you worked up for another round later."

"Probably," he agreed.

When Ray started to try to pull away, I held him closer. "No..." I muttered into his ear. "Not yet." I clung to him as if my life depended on it. I planted kisses on his cheek and tightened my ass around him, not wanting him to end this moment.

"Heh," he grunted. "You want me to get you off, babe?" He reached between us and squeezed a hand around my dick.

I gasped and then cooed at the warm touch. "N-no, baby. It's fine. You don't have to—"

Before I could finish, he was already stroking me. His dick pulsed inside me as he jacked me off. I arched my back within seconds, my hands gripping the sheets. He even thrust back and forth an inch, letting his cocktip rub against my prostate, and I just lay there moaning in ecstasy. "Let me know when you're close, babe," he muttered as his other hand when to pinch my nipple.

I bit my lip and squirmed against him. After a full minute of it, I finally breathed, "Fuck, I'm g-gonna..."

He raked his nails down my chest and stroked my dick

harder and faster. My back arched higher as I howled against the pillow, my seed shooting out and hitting my chin.

"Damn," Ray said with a laugh. "You *were* pent up."

I didn't respond. I was still riding out the waves of pleasure. I had enough awareness to keep my legs locked around his waist, but that was about it.

He leaned forward and licked up the cum trail across my stomach, and I squirmed hard at the ticklish, post-orgasm touch, but he was stronger than me and held me down. Finally, the afterglow passed. I didn't want it to, but it passed.

It was all over.

He smiled up at me as he kissed my lips. He moved to sit up, about to pull out, as he asked, "You want me to grab you a towel while I'm up?" But I didn't have time to even answer.

"Ow!" he yelled as he sat up.

I tried to keep him held close even as he tried to scramble away. My legs kept him locked against me. "Wh-what is it, babe?" I asked. As if I didn't know.

"Hey, let me go, I'm serious. Whizzer," he said, using our safe word.

But I couldn't obey. "No, tell me, what is it? Why don't you want to stay and lie with me a bit longer?"

He struggled again, on the verge of pushing me. "No, seriously, it felt like something just stabbed my dick. Let me pull out real quick."

In the end, I couldn't stop him.

He looked dumbfounded at what he was seeing.

His dick was about a foot away from my asshole at this point, but hundreds of white, silky cords led from my anus to cover his dick. The threads were drawn tight, and he couldn't pull back any further, not without pulling me, too.

"What the fuck?"

I tried to play dumb. Life doesn't prepare you for situations like this. "What do you mean? What's wrong?"

He couldn't look up from the sight to see my face. "Look at this! It's some kind of...rope...or...it's like it's fucking *spiderwebs* or something!"

"No," I muttered, "that can't be it." That was totally it.

He reached down to try to pull at the webs with his hands, but he made no headway. At this point, the threads were pretty much solid. They had started wrapping around his dick the minute he began fucking me. They had lost a lot of their elasticity by now. They didn't even stick to his hands that well.

"The fuck!" he repeated. I was glad he didn't look me in the eye for answers. I wouldn't have had any for him.

I just said, "I'm...I'm so sorry, baby."

Then, he looked up at me. His eyes were wide with fright. I knew he hated spiders, but that's not my fault. Blame fate. Or destiny. Or just downright bad luck. "What? What is it?"

Even as he spoke, *they* came. Tens of spiders crawled from my anus across and through the threads toward his dick. They were black and shiny, like black widows but with smaller bodies and longer legs. They made me do it. They always make me do it. I tried to control their hunger once, but I know now it's just impossible.

Raymond fell backward on his ass at the sight. His balance lost, his torso hung off the end of the bed, but his lower half was still conjoined to mine. His arms spun and flailed, and even out of balance, he was able to tilt his head up and watch as the spiders crawled around his dick and balls, drawing their webbing around him in a tight chastity cage, even as some of the braver spiders stretched their long legs out to pull at his urethra, crawling inside for a warm nap, and maybe, just maybe, a place to lay their eggs.

"I'm so sorry, baby," I repeated. I reached beyond the edge of the bed and grabbed his discarded jockstrap, pulling it up against my nose. My erection came back at the musk, and I focused on jacking off again to ignore the screams a few feet away from me. It was going to be a long night. "I'm so sorry," I said through the green fabric, my cock getting hard again.

KILL IT WITH FIRE

Lube is messy. That's just how it is. Harry and Simon had been fucking for a good two hours already, in a few different positions. They had started against the bookshelf and ended up with Simon tied down spreadeagle on my stomach on the bed. Even after Harry had plowed Simon's ass and bred it nice and deep, the two still weren't done.

There was one major reason for this: Simon wanted to try one of Harry's kinks that he had never done before, wax play. For those who don't know, wax play involves lighting a tapered candle and holding it over your lover's body, letting the hot wax drip onto their skin. For many, this evokes a mix of pain and pleasure. Of course, the closer you hold it to the skin, the hotter and more painful it gets.

While Simon was new to this particular kink, Harry was an experienced pro. He knew exactly what candles to get, how high to hold the candle, and where to let it drip for the greatest balance of pain to pleasure. And Simon trusted Harry when it came to something like this anyway. They had been together for over a year now, and they had already tried a few kinks that were new to at least one of them. Still, it gave Simon a little anxiety. He hated being burned by crackling oil in a skillet; he didn't see the appeal of getting burned for pleasure, even if it didn't leave a mark.

But they had planned it out. They had fucked first, and then Harry had tied Simon face down so that he wouldn't know when or where the wax would fall. He wouldn't be tantalized by watching the drops of wax. He would be facing his pillow, concentrating on breathing and enjoying the sensations. They had established a safe word for the session, and Simon knew it would be okay with Harry if he ended up not liking it. But he still felt a little internal pressure to enjoy the kink. It could be another thing the two of them shared.

"Well, you ready to try this?"

Simon turned his head to look over his shoulder to stare at his lover. While Simon was completely naked, Harry had gotten clothed again in gym shorts and a tank top. Coming out a bad past relationship, Harry had some insecurities about being naked when he wasn't engaging in sex himself. Nevertheless, Simon said, "You look cute."

Harry laughed. "Nah, not half as cute as you. You didn't answer my question."

Simon wagged his ass at Harry. "You're twice as cute as me. And yes, I'm ready. Ready as I can be anyway."

Shaking his head, Harry said, "Alright." He bent over to open the pack of candles he had bought that week. The pack had four candles in it: two black and two red, Simon's favorite colors. Harry broke the plastic wrapping around one of the black ones and set the box aside. Then, he grabbed a paper towel and wrapped it around the base of the candle, so he didn't accidentally drip any wax on himself. Lighting it quickly, he held it in front of his face. It released a thin black smoke into the air, but the candle burned strong, black wax forming around the flame.

He angled it over his right hand and let a drop hit the back of his hand. "Yeah, this isn't too bad," he said, mostly to himself.

Simon responded anyway, "Alright," and he buried his face in the pillow. He wagged his ass again, loving the feeling of Harry's warm seed still deep inside him. The lube covering his ass was still cool against the air, but he felt warm inside. He knew the wax would warm up his skin plenty though. That's part of what he was worried about though, too.

The first drops hit Simon's skin, and he gasped. "Fffuck," he breathed into the pillow.

"You alright?" Harry asked immediately, angling the candle straight again.

"Yeah, just wasn't expecting it."

"Want me to keep going?"

Simon nodded.

Harry raised the candle higher this time and let the black wax drip slowly onto Simon's back. He squirmed with each drop, but Harry noticed that Simon's dick was growing hard between his legs. When Harry had tied Simon down, he had made sure to pull his dick out from under him so he wasn't crushing it (plus it gave Harry a nice view of Simon's balls). But with each drop of wax, Simon's dick grew in size. "Wow, I guess someone is enjoying this."

He lowered the candle a few inches, leaned forward, and shoved two fingers into Simon's still lubed asshole, making the bottom moan into his pillow. The oil-based lube was slick and covered Simon's cheeks and balls. Harry felt Simon's ass clench around his fingers when the candle dripped onto the small of Simon's back. "Good boy," Harry said, standing back. His own shorts were getting a tent in them now. "You're hot like this."

"W-Was that a pun?" Simon managed.

Harry rolled his eyes. "No, goober." He lowered the candle a lot, and Simon really yelped that time. Harry chuckled.

That was when Harry saw the spider dangling in front of his face. It was probably just a common house spider. Its whole body was brown, but it was fairly large—no violin on the back or anything like that. Mostly harmless, but Harry didn't know that. When he saw a spider, his immediate response was, *Kill it.*

The spider was literally just two inches from his nose, its legs waggling in the air. Harry's eyes widened as he tried to swat at the spider suddenly to get it away from his face. Swatting at it was instinctive. He didn't use logic or reason to do it. He just reacted. It was, pun intended, the heat of the moment. In using the candle hand to swat at it, he sent a stream of wax spilling onto Simon's lower back.

"*Ah! Fuck!*" Simon yelled, struggling violently with the restraints.

"Oh, shit!" Harry managed, holding the candle upright again and putting a hand on Simon. "I'm so sorry. Are you okay?"

Simon hissed breath and shivered. "Y-Yeah, what the

fuck was that for?"

"Sorry. There was a spider, and I had to swat it. The fucker was just dangling in front of my face. It was just like muscle reflex. I'm so sorry, babe."

"Ah, it's okay."

Harry looked down at the line of black wax on Simon's back. "Are you sure you're alright? That looks like it could have really not felt good."

"Yeah, not...my favorite part, but we were good up till that."

"Ok," Harry said, exhaling. "Want me to keep going, or do you want to take a break?"

"I'm fine to keep going." He wagged his ass again, a little more shakily this time. "If you're good now?"

"Y-Yeah," Harry managed. He looked down at the bed to see if he could see where the spider went. He knew he had to have hit it. He just didn't know where it went off to. The sheets were light brown, but that spider had been fairly dark. It should have stood right out. But it was nowhere to be found. He risked a glance upward at the ceiling, scared he might see a hundred of the tiny fuckers nesting up above him, but there was nothing there either. He shivered despite himself. "Yeah, I'm good. Was looking for where the fucker went, but in any case, he's gone now." He shook his head once and then said, "Okay, here we go again."

And he continued dripping wax down Simon's back. After a couple minutes, he moved down to drip wax onto Simon's thighs. That really made Simon squirm, but Harry only heard pleasant yelps. Twice, he even dared to drip wax onto Simon's cock and balls. The yelps became moans at that point.

"Very good boy," Harry said, fondling his own erection

through his gym shorts. "Very good boy indeed. You'll get a treat later."

"Oh yeah, sir? What's that?" Simon said through the pillow.

Harry smirked. "Oh, I have a few ideas at least."

Simon wagged his ass once more, and Harry dripped wax onto his asscrack. "Yeah, keep tempting me with that ass, and you'll see sooner than you thought you would, pup."

He held the candle lower to Simon's skin, letting the wax drip down his ass cheeks and onto his thighs and balls. Simon jerked each time a drop hit his skin this close, but he never used the safe word. Even though the pain increased with each drop of hot wax, so did the pleasure.

After another five minutes of the concentrated wax play, Harry stood up fully and straightened the candle. "Alright, babe, I think I'm about done. What do you say?"

"Sure, daddy," Simon said, his body very visibly relaxing.

"Heh, and then I can give you your treat since you've been so good." Harry looked into the flame on the tip of the candle. It had only burned off an inch or so of the candle. But he had definitely done a good job. There was so much black wax on Simon's backside that it looked like he had black ink splattered over him at points. It wasn't Harry's longest wax play session, but it was probably his most enjoyable one, sans spider.

"Yes please. Are you going to untie me first? Wrists are a bit sore."

"Oh, of course, babe!" Harry said.

He was just about to blow out the candle, but

something stopped him suddenly that he did not expect.

When he felt something on the back of his hand, he angled it toward his face, not caring that it deposited another thick stream of hot wax onto Simon's balls, eliciting Simon's loudest scream yet, and saw where the spider had gone after all. Staring back at him with six eyes was the missing creature.

"*Holy fucking shit!*" Harry yelled himself as he flung the candle and spider away from him. The spider landed on the center of Simon's back. The candle, however, fell between Simon's legs.

You have to understand. What Harry just felt was a full-body visceral experience. Seeing a spider on his actual person, he felt violated. Realizing that spider had been there for at least a few minutes upset him deeply. With this knowledge, it might not come as a surprise as he ran screaming out of the bedroom, horrified.

Simon's pain from the hot wax was mostly over, now that the initial shock was over. He had no idea what had just happened. He didn't see any of it. But he did feel the lit candle roll under his balls. As bad as that heat was, as his pubic hairs began igniting, things got exponentially worse when the fire caught the oil-based lube (which, it turns out, is actually quite flammable), and his lower backside erupted in fire.

The spider, scared of the rising heat, scuttled away.

Simon, however, struggled frantically against his bindings, screaming from just the scorching pain as his balls and ass erupted in flames, the fires slowly working their way up the rest of his body.

Harry, on the other hand, had never stopped running. Simon heard his screams only in the first five or six seconds. Then, Harry's screams were cut off abruptly by the door slamming on his way out of the apartment. Harry had left the building, and Harry had no idea what had happened to Simon.

Even when the smoke alarm went off in their apartment, and the siren went off for the whole building, Harry was confident it couldn't have been their apartment. He was sure the candle had to have went out when he threw it. Surely, the wind from that throw had extinguished the flame. Yeah, Simon was tied down, but this would only take a couple minutes. Right? After five minutes outside with everyone else waiting for the fire truck, he worked his way around the building where there was a window into his apartment. It was covered in smoke and fire.

"Oh shit..." Harry said. If Harry had been an animal, a weasel, let's say, his ears would have flattened, and his tail would have gone between his legs.

Near the window, too small for Harry to see, the spider escaped through a crack between the wall and the glass, leaving the heat and smoke behind, and seeking new shelter in the bushes.

Inside the apartment, Simon's screams continued, even as his balls made an audible pop in the spreading fire.

ALWAYS WASH YOUR TOYS BETWEEN USES

When your lover of two years asks if you want to try on an old chastity cage he's had hiding in his closet for about five years, you ask the obvious questions: Where did Leon get it? Who was it for? Is that something he's into?

When he responds, "Got it online when I was with my ex. Yeah, I like putting a guy in chastity. I think it's hot. But there's no pressure if that's not something you're into," you might actually be interested. Your interest might verge on arousal. He pulls it out, and it looks fine. It looks clean. It's pure steel or whatever, so it doesn't rust, at least not noticeably. Within seconds of taking it out, Leon is kissing you. He says, "So, what do you think? Wanna try it?"

"Um...for how long?" you ask.

"Well, people do it for different lengths of time. An hour. A day. A week."

"How about a month?" you ask. You have no reason to

suspect you can do it for a whole month, but you like a good challenge. The worst you'll feel is discomfort, you know. So, what the hell? Why not be adventurous? Dive right in and all.

"A month? You want to start off with a full month? From the get-go?"

"Sure," you find yourself saying. "But afterward, we're having a sex marathon, got it?"

Leon laughs. "Fuck yeah. I'm down for all of this." He kisses you again. "Well, if we're gonna do this, let's at least do it in better lighting." He grabs your hand and pulls you out of the bedroom and into the kitchen. Your bedroom is mostly lit by just a lamp, but the apartment kitchen has those glaring white fluorescents you've always hated. Still, he's right. It's definitely the brightest part of the place.

Once there, he pulls your pants down, and you gasp. You lean back against the kitchen counter as he gets on his knees and takes your cock into his mouth.

"Wh-What are you doing that for?" you ask.

"Hey," he says, between sucks, "it'll be the most action you get for a little while. Plus, it's nice to tease you before we lock you up."

Just when you're semihard, he unlocks the cage he had dug out of the closet and pushes the metal ring over your dick. He sucks you again while he pulls your balls through the ring. Next, he pulls his mouth off your dick with an audible *pop* and pushes the main metal cage over your cock. This is your first time seeing it up close. It's fully enclosed, looking more like a curved PVC pipe than a piece of sex gear. Since you're semihard, the cage fits very tight. But the lube of Leon's saliva gets it all the way on without pinching your base or anything.

The lock clicks into place.

"How does it feel?" Leon asks.

You move your hips back and forth testing the weight. It's heavy, but it's tight. There's no way it could just fall off or anything. It's on there until it's unlocked. "Feels okay. I like how tight it is. Feels like there's someone just holding my dick, like I'm being teased long-term or something."

"Good!" Leon says as he leans forward to suck on your balls. "I'm going to enjoy really teasing you over the next few weeks then.

Then begins your month in chastity.

At first, it's pretty easy. It's a metal weight between your legs, so it's hard not to notice, but you get used to the weight pretty quickly. Since the cage is curved, it's impossible to get "uncomfortably hard," despite Leon's constant teasing. He plays with your nipples some nights, sucks your balls others. Sometimes, he sits on your face and makes you rim him. And sometimes, he just lifts your legs over his shoulders and fucks you. And the cage feels like a comfy little tease. You have a strong feeling in that first week that it's going to feel nice when you get to cum finally.

But after the first week, you notice this strong itching sensation. Your balls itch a bit, but it's mostly your caged cock. Since there are no openings except for the urethra, there's no real way for you to scratch that itch. One day, while Leon was at work, you even took the kitchen sink spray nozzle to try to spray into the cage to see if that would help. Nothing. And rather than the itching going away after a couple of days, it got increasingly worse until it began to just hurt.

After the second week, the feeling did go away. It

seemed rather sudden, but it felt like *all* feeling was gone. The itching was gone, but so was the feeling of pleasure when Leon teased you and even that pleasant feeling of heat when you piss. In fact, the first time you noticed it, you were half-awake and trying to pee but couldn't actually do it until you focused and realized you had peed (and missed the toilet wildly) and just couldn't feel that you had.

It all felt wrong. Your first instinct was that maybe the cage wasn't all steel like Leon had said. Maybe there was a metal alloy in it that you were actually allergic to. That would explain the itching and now the numbness. With a sigh, you make the decision at least.

You just can't take it anymore. It has to come off. Your own pride be damned, the cage has to come off.

You try to mess with it yourself first, while Leon is at work. You look around for where he might have hidden the keys to the lock. You check the bondage drawer of your dresser, Leon's computer desk, and even the miscellaneous drawer in the kitchen. Nothing.

Then, you think maybe with enough soap you might be able to get it off yourself. You get in the shower, pour soap all around it, especially around your balls, but nothing. It won't budge.

"Fuck," you whine in exasperation.

After rinsing off, you hear the door to the apartment close and Leon yell out, "Honey, I'm home."

You step out of the shower and dry off. "In the bathroom, babe. When you get settled, I need to talk to you about something." Red flushes in your face. You feel like you're quitting even suggesting taking the cage off. But you're genuinely worried. What if the cage comes off, and your skin is just covered in boils from the allergy? What if it's bruised all over from the cage being too tight? Your mind imagines the worst. But none of it hurts in the moment as much as your pride at not being good enough at your lover's fetish. You're terrified you'll somehow disappoint him by asking to take it off. But you tough it out and exit the bathroom. Leon is waiting at the door, a worried look on his face now.

"Well, what is it, babe?" he says.

You lower your eyes. "Well, it's about the chastity cage."

"Yeah? What about it?" He looks down at the metal trap between your legs with a smile.

"I think I need it to come off."

The smile fades off Leon's face, but his immediate response is, "Sure, I can take it off. Is everything okay?"

You're a bit hurt that it was so easy for him to be okay with taking it off, as if you weren't hopeful it could be a kink you two could share. But you know he will be fine with it, even if you're a bit upset by it.

"Yeah," you say. "It just...um...I think I might be allergic? All last week, it was itching like hell, and this week, my dick just feels...numb. Like I can't feel anything down there."

"Oh really?" he says in disbelief. He reaches forward and strokes your balls teasingly.

You purse your lips and just shake your head. "Nothing. I don't even feel your hand there."

Leon blinks. "Um, yeah, that's not great."

"Yeah...can you take it off? I don't know where the key is."

"Yeah, ok, let me go get it. It's just on the bookshelf by the dresser."

You roll your eyes. Of course it would be on one of

your countless bookshelves. You didn't even think to look there.

As Leon comes back to the living room with the keys, he says, "Why didn't you tell me about this sooner? I wouldn't have minded checking for you or anything. I hope you're not allergic."

"I..." you start. "I was nervous. I know this is something you enjoy, so I wanted to enjoy it too. I didn't want you to see me as a quitter or anything." You're practically on the verge of tears. You're just so embarrassed. You're embarrassed by your inability to go through with the full month, and you're just as embarrassed that you've been stubborn enough to wait till now to communicate your discomfort.

"Whoa, whoa, it's fine, babe. I don't see you as a quitter or anything at all. I just care about you. I don't want you getting hurt, not over something like this. Okay?"

"Okay, love," you say, thinking to yourself that you don't deserve such a perfect guy.

"Alright, let's get this cage off you."

"Yes please. Wanna do it over in the chair?"

"Uh, sure," he says, and you hold his hand.

With an anxious nod, Leon guides you to a chair, and he helps pull your pants down to your ankles. He gets a playful grin and even noses your cage through the jockstrap, but you just don't even feel it. He frowns suddenly. "I don't want to sound rude myself, babe, but you smell bad."

"Huh? I just got out of the shower. I dumped like a third a bottle of handsoap on that. How could it smell bad?"

"Well, it...it smells like our soap yeah, but it smells like something died and just rolled in the soap."

Your frown matches his. "Let's just hurry up. Get it over with. Take it off."

"Ok, babe." He pushes the key in the lock, twists it, and the lock pops off. Leon places it on the table beside you and then looks down at your balls. "Babe... your balls...it's like there's movement in them." You look down and notice it too. Like there's something inside trying to get out. Leon starts working the cage. It seems stuck at first, and then it finally gives.

The cage slips off, and the reeking musk of decaying flesh knocks Leon onto his ass. Even you have to cover your nose from the stench. Down between your legs is a gray mass of flesh. There are no blisters, boils, or bruises like you thought, but covering your dick are thick sheets of spider webs. They wrap around your cock in the exact shape of the chastity cage, keeping it at the exact same size and shape it was when Leon put it on you. Millimeter-round holes dot your cock, where little brown spiders crawl in and out of hiding. The holes are laced with webbing, and some of the spiders sit in wait inside these funnels, staring up at you with black, beady eyes. Many of the others travel between holes and work on strengthening the web. Legs poke out from your urethra as a larger spider pushes itself out to walk on the underside of your dick.

Leon screams and crawls backward at the sight. You can't believe it. You don't even feel it as the spiders scuttle in, on, and through your penis, sustained by the flesh inside. They're just going about their day, regardless of the fact that that is a part of your body.

"What the fuck?" you say in disbelief.

"H-How the fuck did that happen?" Leon asks, keeping his distance from you.

"Was...was there a spider in the chastity cage?"

Leon's jaw drops, and he shakes his head in disbelief. "I...I didn't check. I just...assumed..."

You're shaking your head now too.

You reach down with a shaking hand as if to cradle your dick in horror, and somehow this singular touch is the straw that breaks the camel's back. Your cock falls off your body, sending many of the spiders that resided within it scuttling across your living room carpet. But in the hole where your dick and balls once were, thousands of tiny black babies scurry around, a living, writhing mass of hair, legs, eyes, and more eggs, pulsating inside your flesh. They crawl deeper inside you, hiding from the light.

Jonathan W. Thurston is a gay, HIV-positive writer in Lansing, Michigan. His previous book, *Straight Men*, was recommended for an ALAA Over the Rainbow award and a Lambda Literary Award, and also heavily praised by Publishers Weekly. He has also delved into nonfiction with *Blood Criminals: Living with HIV in 21st Century America* through Weasel Press.

Other Titles by this Author

Blood Criminals: Living with HIV in the 21st Century America
Celibate Men
The Devil Has a Black Dog
Straight Men

Other Books from Sinister Stoat Press

The City Around the World by Elliot Harper
The Last Book You'll Ever Read by Scott Hughes
Body & Blood edited by Weasel
Carnage by Weasel
Dread edited by Weasel
Ghostly Pornographers by Thomas White